神 白馬
图 马与

The Horse and
the Mysterious
Drawing

This book is edited and designed by the Editorial Committee of *Cultural China* series

Story and Illustrations: Li Jian
Translation: Yijin Wert

Copy Editor: Susan Luu Xiang
Editor: Yang Xiaohe
Editorial Director: Zhang Yicong

Senior Consultants: Sun Yong, Wu Ying, Yang Xinci
Managing Director and Publisher: Wang Youbu

ISBN: 978-1-60220-984-8

Address any comments about *The Horse and the Mysterious Drawing* to:

Better Link Press
99 Park Ave
New York, NY 10016
USA

or

Shanghai Press and Publishing Development Company
F 7 Donghu Road, Shanghai, China (200031)
Email: comments_betterlinkpress@hotmail.com

Printed in China by Shenzhen Donnelley Printing Co., Ltd.

1 3 5 7 9 10 8 6 4 2

The Horse and the Mysterious Drawing

A Story in English and Chinese
by Li Jian

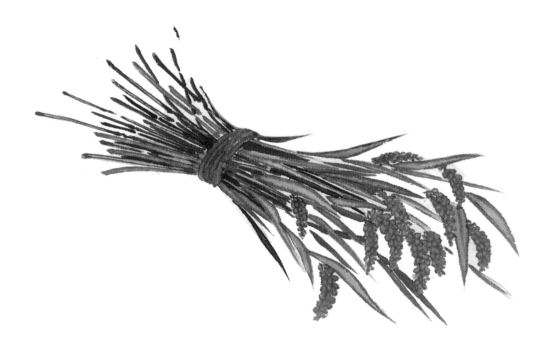

Better Link Press

很久以前在中国的黄河边，住着一个叫阿福的男孩。他和家人靠采野果子和打猎为生。

Long long ago by the Yellow River in China, there was a boy named Ah Fu. He and his family lived off the land. They hunted and gathered wild fruits.

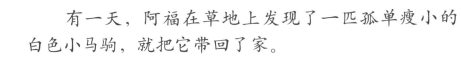

有一天，阿福在草地上发现了一匹孤单瘦小的白色小马驹，就把它带回了家。

One day, Ah Fu brought home a lonely and skinny little white pony that he found on the grassland.

尽管食物来之不易，但阿福总会省下一些给小马驹。小马驹渐渐长成了一匹高大健壮的白马，它也成为了阿福最好的朋友。

Although it was very hard for him to find food, Ah Fu always made sure to save some for the pony. That is how the little pony became a big strong horse. It also became Ah Fu's best friend.

当他们在田野里找食物时，阿福发现白马很爱吃一种植物的穗。他很好奇，就带了一些回家。

While they were looking for food in the field, Ah Fu noticed that the white horse loved to eat the ears of one particular plant. He became so curious that he brought some home.

阿福的妈妈把壳去掉，用水煮成了粥。他们全家都觉得粥的味道很好，就给这种植物起名叫粟。

"要是能耕种并收获足够的粟米，我们就再也不用为食物发愁了。"阿福想。

Ah Fu's Mom removed the husks and used water to cook a porridge. They all thought the porridge was very delicious, so gave the plant a name and called it millet.

"If we can grow millet at every harvest, we will never have to worry about food," Ah Fu thought.

可是，阿福和家人都不会种田。他们播下的种子不是不发芽，就是被冻死，收获的东西还不够全家吃一顿的。

Unfortunately, Ah Fu and his family didn't know how to farm. Some of the seeds they planted did not sprout. Some died of the cold weather. What they got at the end of the season could barely make a full meal for the family.

阿福非常苦恼。

"明天黄河里会出现一件宝贝，"一天白马对阿福说，
"如果我们能得到它，就能解决你的问题。"

Ah Fu was very much troubled by the problem.

"A treasure will appear in the Yellow River tomorrow,"
his white horse said to him one day, "If we can get that
treasure, your problem will be solved."

第二天，白马带阿福来到黄河边，它眼睛一眨不眨地盯着河水。当河水开始剧烈翻滚时，白马突然纵身跳进黄河，不见了踪影。

The next day, the white horse brought Ah Fu to the Yellow River.
It stared at the river without blinking its eyes. When the river started
to tumble, it suddenly jumped into the Yellow River and disappeared.

没过多久，白马又奇迹般从河水中跳了出来，它全身上下没被打湿，背上的马毛却形成了一幅由黑白斑点组成的图。

After a little while, the white horse miraculously jumped out of the water. Its body was still dry, but there was a drawing made of black and white dots on its back.

这张图就是白马所说的宝贝！可是，阿福一点也看不懂。

"宝图里蕴含了季节周期的规律。"白马对阿福说，"如果顺应变化耕种，就能事半功倍；如果逆反规律耕种，就会事倍功半，甚至一无所获。"

This drawing was the treasure the white horse had told Ah Fu about! Unfortunately, Ah Fu could not understand the meaning of it.

"This drawing explains the natural cycles of the seasons," the white horse began to tell Ah Fu, "If we farm by following the seasonal cycles, we will succeed without much trouble. But if we farm against them, we will fail no matter how hard we work."

阿福想成为一个成功的农民。他按照白
马告诉自己的自然规律耕种。

Ah Fu wanted to be a successful farmer.
He followed the rules of nature as the white
horse had explained to him.

当天上春雷响动、冬眠动物苏醒、大地回暖时，"到翻耕田地的时候了，"白马告诉阿福。

When the thunder roared, the animals were awakened from hibernating and the earth turned warm, "it's time to plow your fields," the white horse told Ah Fu.

当雨水增多、水塘出现浮萍时，白马告诉阿福："到了播种的时候了。"

"It's time to plant seeds," the white horse told Ah Fu when it started to rain often, and duckweed was floating upon the ponds.

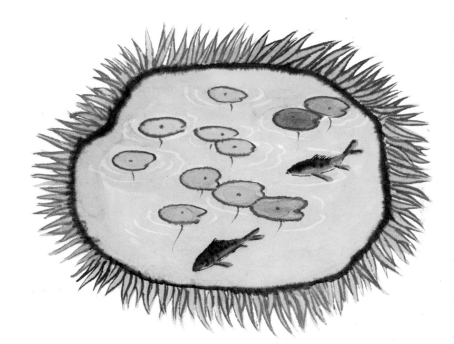

当天气炎热、蟋蟀鸣叫时，白马告诉阿福：
"到了灌溉的时候了。"

"It's time to water the plants," the white horse
told Ah Fu on sunny days when the crickets chirped.

当蝉不再鸣叫、大雁向南飞时，白马告诉阿福："到了收割的时候了。"

"It's time for harvest," the white horse told Ah Fu when the cicadas stopped their chirping and the wild geese flew south.

当河水结冰时，白马告诉阿福："到了让土地休养的时候了。"

"It's time to let the earth rest," the white horse told Ah Fu when the rivers started to freeze.

连续几年，阿福全家都获得了大丰收，丰衣足食。

Year after year, Ah Fu and his family had bountiful harvests and lived a happy and contented life.

阿福把耕种的知识教给了村子里的乡亲。一传十、十传百，从此人们开始跟着季节规律耕种。

Ah Fu then started to teach the farmers in his village about farming. This knowledge was passed on from one person to another. From then on, people started to farm by following the rules of the seasons.

后来，聪明的人们把这些知识总结成了"二十四节气"，还为每个节气取了名字。

Later, people who had a lot of experience wrote down their observations in the "24 solar terms" and gave a special name to each of them.

24 Solar Terms

English	Chinese	Date
Start of Spring	立春	Feb 4 or 5
Rain Water	雨水	Feb 19 or 20
Awakening of Insects	惊蛰	Mar 6 or 5
Vernal Equinox	春分	Mar 21 or 20
Clear and Bright	清明	Apr 5 or 6
Grain Rain	谷雨	Apr 20 or 21
Start of Summer	立夏	May 6 or 5
Grain Full	小满	May 21 or 22
Grain in Ear	芒种	Jun 6 or 7
Summer Solstice	夏至	Jun 22 or 21
Slight Heat	小暑	Jul 7 or 8
Severe Heat	大暑	Jul 23 or 24
Start of Autumn	立秋	Aug 8 or 7
End of Heat	处暑	Aug 23 or 24
White Dew	白露	Sep 8 or 7
Autumnal Equinox	秋分	Sep 23 or 24
Cold Dew	寒露	Oct 8 or 9
Frost Descent	霜降	Oct 24 or 23
Start of Winter	立冬	Nov 8 or 7
Light Snow	小雪	Nov 23 or 22
Heavy Snow	大雪	Dec 7 or 8
Winter Solstice	冬至	Dec 22 or 23
Slight Cold	小寒	Jan 6 or 5
Severe Cold	大寒	Jan 20 or 21

直到今天，二十四节气的知识还在指导着人们的生活。

Even until now, the 24 solar terms still guide the lives of the people.